For my nephews, Forrest and Guillermo

Balzer + Bray is an imprint of HarperCollins Publishers.

Hush, Little Bunny
Copyright © 2019 by David Ezra Stein
Hand lettering by Leah Palmer Preiss
All rights reserved. Manufactured in China.
www.harpercollinschildrens.com

Library of Congress Control Number: 2018933140
ISBN 978-0-06-284522-1

The artist used mixed media on watercolor paper to create the illustrations for this book.
Typography by Dana Fritts
18 19 20 21 22 SCP 10 9 8 7 6 5 4 3 2 1

First Edition

DAVID EZRA STEIN

Hush, Little Bunny

BALZER + BRAY
An Imprint of HarperCollinsPublishers

Come, little bunny, don't be shy.

It's time to tell the snow goodbye.

Hush, little bunny, don't you cry.

Papa's gonna give you the big blue sky.

And if that big blue sky clouds over,

Papa's gonna give you a patch of clover.

And when that patch of clover is done,

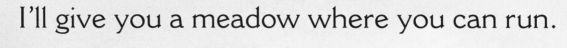
I'll give you a meadow where you can run.

And if a hawk comes gliding down,

I'll show you a nest safe underground.

And when that hiding place gets tight,

I'll take you back into the light.

And if the afternoon brings showers,

we'll stay by a tree that's hung with flowers.

And when those flowers blow away,

we'll find some other bunnies and play.

And if those bunnies don't play fair,

I'll growl at them just like a bear.

Hush, little bunny, don't you cry.

Papa's gonna show you a firefly.

And if that firefly takes wing,

I'll take you where the blackbird sings.

And when the sun is sinking fast,

we'll tunnel softly through the grass.

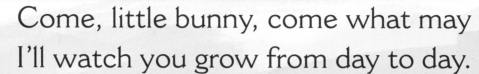

Come, little bunny, come what may
I'll watch you grow from day to day.

And when the spring has come and gone,
I'm still gonna love you all year long.